RUBY CELEBRATES!
The Hanukkah Hunt

Laura Gehl

illustrated by
Olga and Aleksey Ivanov

Albert Whitman & Company
Chicago, Illinois

"Let's add more glitter," Ruby says, trying to cheer up her cousin Avital.

But even after the Hanukkah cards are covered in blue and silver sparkles, Avital doesn't smile.

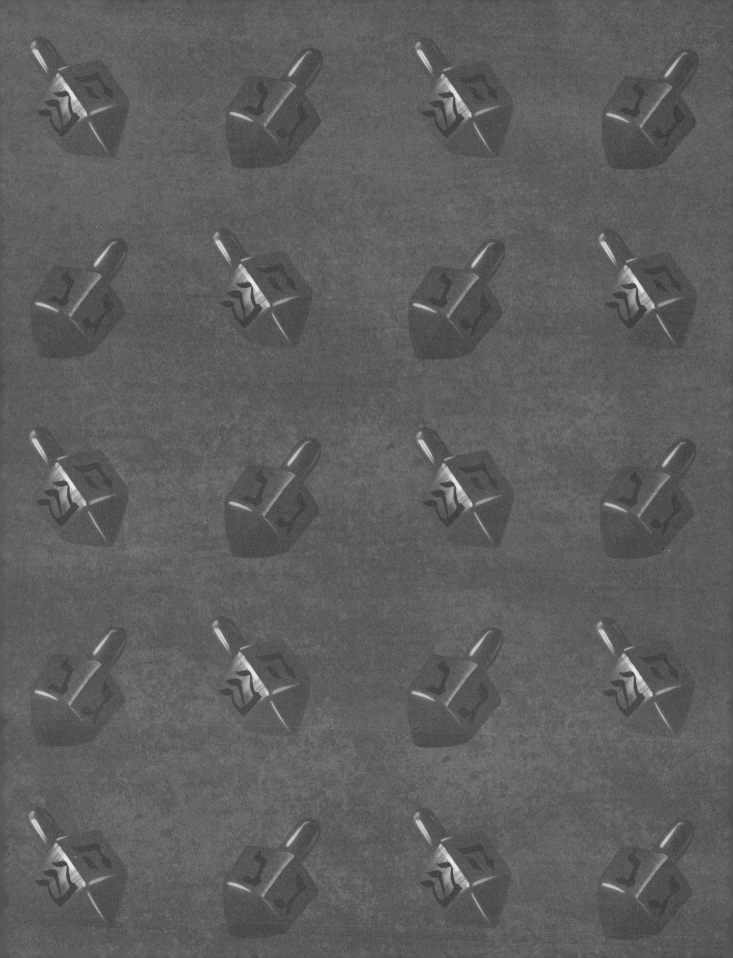

Avital doesn't smile when Ruby's dad offers her a freshly baked dreidel-shaped cookie either.

Or when flour-covered Benny pretends to be a ghost, shouting, "Boo!"

After Avital goes home, Dad tells Ruby that Avital's mom has to go on a big trip for work—and she's going to miss Hanukkah.

Now Ruby understands why Avital was sad. Aunt Deb makes the very best latkes—even better than Bubbe's. She also plays the guitar when the family sings "Maoz Tzur" and "I Have a Little Dreidel." Hanukkah won't be as much fun without her. Especially for Avital.

"I'm going to ask everyone to help me make a huge eight-night Hanukkah treasure hunt for Avital," Ruby tells Dad. "That way she will have a happy Hanukkah even with her mom away."

Ruby decides that Avital should get a big, exciting gift at the
very end of the treasure hunt, on the last night of Hanukkah.
And she knows exactly what that big, exciting gift should be...

"Can we get Avital a kitten?" Ruby asks Avital's dad, Uncle Will.
"Cats are easy to take care of. And sweet. And cuddly. A kitten would
bring YEARS of happiness!"

"Sorry, Ruby," Uncle Will says. "Aunt Deb and I have our hands full right now with Baby Ellie. She's sweet and cuddly too. But NOT easy to take care of."

On the first night of Hanukkah, right after the family lights the menorah, Ruby reads Avital the first clue.

For movie night
when kids need a bite

"'Movie night'...'a bite'...hmm. Oh, I know! It's Uncle Jake's popcorn machine!"

Uncle Will escorts Ruby and Avital to Uncle Jake's house.

Avital reaches inside the popcorn popper. "A bag of gelt! Yum! And a new dreidel!"

The next night, Ruby reads Avital the second clue.

I go bow wow wow.
Come find me right now.

"Oh, Boaz!" Avital says with a laugh. "That one was too easy!"

Sure enough, when they arrive at Cousin Ethan's house, Boaz is wearing something different from his usual collar.

"A necklace!" Avital shouts. "It's so pretty!"

"My moms helped me make it," Ethan replies proudly.

Ruby notices Avital's smile slip away. She wonders if Avital is remembering that her own mom won't be back until Hanukkah is over.

When Avital goes to look in the mirror, Ethan whispers to Ruby, "Did you think of a big surprise for the end of the treasure hunt?"

"No," Ruby says with a groan. "Uncle Will said 'no' to a kitten, and I can't think of anything else good enough!"

On the third night, after eating sufganiyot at Avital's house, Ruby reads the next clue.

Under the bed
for the tiniest head

"My dolls have tiny heads," Avital thinks out loud. "But they don't have beds."

"Besides the dolls, who has the smallest head in our family?" Ruby asks.

"Baby Ellie!" Avital yells, racing upstairs to look under Ellie's crib. "Ooh! Sparkly markers!"

For the next three nights, Ruby is glad to see Avital grinning and laughing as she follows the clues and collects her gifts...

But Avital's smile disappears whenever she thinks about her mom missing the fun. And Ruby *still* doesn't know what the big, exciting gift for the last night of Hanukkah should be.

On the seventh night, after Uncle Will uses the shamash to light seven candles, Ruby reads Avital the second-to-last clue.

I'm heavy and blue.

I hold a hammer or two.

"Hmm…could it be Great-Uncle Fred's toolbox?" Avital guesses.

Avital looks in the toolbox and finds a set of ceramic animals nestled inside. "Ducks!" she exclaims, hugging Great-Uncle Fred. "My favorite! Thank you!"

Nearby, Great-Aunt Rosa puts down her phone and beckons Ruby over. "I just heard some good news," she says.

After Great-Aunt Rosa explains, Ruby finally knows *exactly* what the big, exciting surprise at the end of the treasure hunt should be!

The next night at Ruby's house, she reads Avital the final clue.

I'm too big for just a broom.

I'm the size of a whole room.

"Too big for a broom? I don't get it!" Avital says.

"Where do you keep the brooms at your house?" Ruby asks.

"In the closet," Avital says. "Oh! A closet the size of a room? I know! It's the walk-in closet at Bubbe and Zayde's house! Let's go!"

Avital runs into the house and makes a beeline for the walk-in closet. Ruby can't wait to see Avital's face.

Avital throws open the closet door, and...

"Happy Hanukkah, sweetheart! I was able to come home early! I even made latkes!"

"Now we have a surprise for you, Ruby," says Aunt Deb. "To say thank you for making Hanukkah so much fun for Avital."

"Someone told me cats are easy to take care of. And sweet. And cuddly," Uncle Will says with a smile.

"I heard they bring years of happiness," Dad adds.

Ruby pets the kitten's soft fur, her face glowing brighter than the Hanukkah candles. "This one definitely will."

Benny runs over to show their new pet his favorite four-sided top. "Dreidel!" he shouts.

Ruby laughs. "Benny, I think you just named our new kitten. Welcome to the family, Dreidel!"

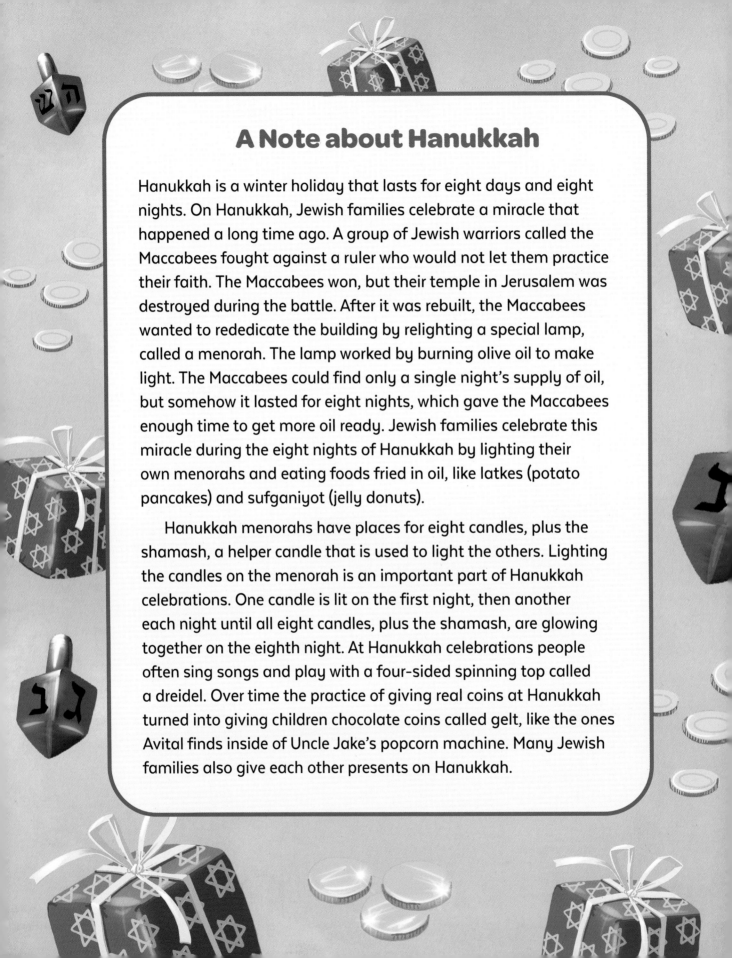

A Note about Hanukkah

Hanukkah is a winter holiday that lasts for eight days and eight nights. On Hanukkah, Jewish families celebrate a miracle that happened a long time ago. A group of Jewish warriors called the Maccabees fought against a ruler who would not let them practice their faith. The Maccabees won, but their temple in Jerusalem was destroyed during the battle. After it was rebuilt, the Maccabees wanted to rededicate the building by relighting a special lamp, called a menorah. The lamp worked by burning olive oil to make light. The Maccabees could find only a single night's supply of oil, but somehow it lasted for eight nights, which gave the Maccabees enough time to get more oil ready. Jewish families celebrate this miracle during the eight nights of Hanukkah by lighting their own menorahs and eating foods fried in oil, like latkes (potato pancakes) and sufganiyot (jelly donuts).

Hanukkah menorahs have places for eight candles, plus the shamash, a helper candle that is used to light the others. Lighting the candles on the menorah is an important part of Hanukkah celebrations. One candle is lit on the first night, then another each night until all eight candles, plus the shamash, are glowing together on the eighth night. At Hanukkah celebrations people often sing songs and play with a four-sided spinning top called a dreidel. Over time the practice of giving real coins at Hanukkah turned into giving children chocolate coins called gelt, like the ones Avital finds inside of Uncle Jake's popcorn machine. Many Jewish families also give each other presents on Hanukkah.

Let's Play Dreidel!

You'll need:

A dreidel

Family or friends

10 pennies or gelt for each player

1. Each player starts with ten pennies and puts one of them in the middle of the table.

2. Starting with the youngest person and moving clockwise, each player spins the dreidel when it is their turn.

3. If the dreidel lands on "shin (שׁ)," the player puts another penny in the middle.

4. If the dreidel lands on "nun (נ)" nothing happens.

5. If the dreidel lands on "he (ה)," the player gets to take half the pennies from the middle, rounding up if there is an odd number.

6. If the dreidel lands on "gimel (ג)," the player gets to take all the pennies from the middle. After one player gets a gimel, every player again puts one penny into the middle.

7. Keep playing until one player has ALL the pennies!

The four Hebrew letters on the dreidel (nun, gimel, he, and shin) stand for, "Nes gadol haya sham," which means, "A great miracle happened there."

For Ruth and Eva, with lots of love—LG

To all children, who like to celebrate!—OI & AI

Library of Congress Cataloging-in-Publication data
is on file with the publisher.

Text copyright © 2022 by Laura Gehl
Illustrations copyright © 2022 by Albert Whitman & Company
Illustrations by Olga and Aleksey Ivanov
First published in the United States of America in 2022 by Albert Whitman & Company
ISBN 978-0-8075-7175-0 (hardcover)
ISBN 978-0-8075-7179-8 (ebook)

Printed in China
10 9 8 7 6 5 4 3 2 1 WKT 26 25 24 23 22

For more information about Albert Whitman & Company,
visit our website at www.albertwhitman.com.